THE
ACCIDENTAL ANARCHIST

This title is number three in the Frayed Edge Press Street Smart Series

Other titles in the series include:

Full Fare by Jean-Bernard Pouy

Down and Out in Paris, with Cat by R. A. Bolo

Stealing MacGuffin by Matthew Kastel

Pele's Domain by Albert Tucher

THE ACCIDENTAL ANARCHIST

A. R. Melnik

Frayed Edge Press
Philadelphia, PA

Publishers Cataloging-in-Publication Data

Names: Melnik, Anastazia.
Title: The accidental anarchist / A.R. Melnik.
Description: Philadelphia, PA : Frayed Edge Press, 2019. | Series: Street smart series ; 3 | Summary: Middle-aged English professor Caroline Wilson impulsively boards a commuter bus to New York one morning. A turn down a New York City alley unexpectedly plunges her into a world she never could have imagined, where young anarchists are battling against human traffickers—and they need Caroline's help.
Identifiers: LCCN 2019946859 | ISBN 9781642510157 (pbk.) | ISBN 9781642510164 (ebook)
Subjects: LCSH: Anarchists--Fiction. | College teachers--Fiction. | Human trafficking --Fiction. | New York (N.Y.)--Fiction. | BISAC: FICTION / City Life. | FICTION / Political. | FICTION / Thrillers Crime.
Classification: LCC PS3613.E46 A3 2019 | DDC 843 M4--dc23
LC record available at https://lccn.loc.gov/2019946859

For Cleyre

Caroline was already beginning to question the wisdom of this trip.

By most people's standards, it was a fairly quick one—Philadelphia is only two hours from New York City, whether you go by car, train, or bus. She'd chosen the commuter bus because it had free wifi, unlike the train, and she could work on her laptop on the way up and back. There was no driving or parking to worry about. It was not just quick, but quick and easy.

She'd chosen to do this: a spur of the moment get-away, just by herself, up to New York and back in one day. But it was already starting to bother her, wiggling like a loose tooth that just won't let you forget it. She kept turning over in her mind the various worst-case scenarios of what could possibly go wrong. She imagined James getting a phone call from a hospital in New York, where she'd been taken after a vicious subway knife attack. "No," he'd say, "you must be mistaken. My wife isn't in New York." Or the news headline, days later: "Dismembered body identified as that of missing Philadelphia woman."

She took a deep breath and tried to put these gruesome thoughts out of her mind. "I've been to New York a million times," she exaggerated, "and nothing's ever gone wrong. And if it does, I've got my cell phone. I can call someone." Who she'd call, she wasn't sure. James would still be in Philly, two hours away from helping her. She vaguely knew a few people in New York, but she didn't even have their phone numbers with her.

"What was I thinking?" she asked herself as the double-decker commuter bus pulled away from the curb and started rounding 30th Street Station. She'd left the house an hour earlier, just like she was heading to campus on any other day. She had her backpack with laptop, books, and papers slung over one shoulder, and she'd called out "See you tonight!" to James as she held the front door halfway open. "See ya!" he'd called back, just like any other day. She'd walked as usual to the trolley stop three blocks away and waited for the trolley to arrive. But instead of getting off at her usual stop, she'd stayed on for a few additional stops and gotten off at 30th Street. Hoping she wouldn't run into anyone she knew, she'd quickly headed to the side street across from the train station, where the commuter bus companies picked up passengers. She'd lingered in front of the bus with the "New York City" sign above, until the driver had called, "Hey, lady! You gettin' on or what?" The exchange of a twenty-dollar bill and a paper ticket happened quickly. It had all seemed so easy.

But now she was starting to feel anxious, maybe a six on a scale of one to ten. Maybe a seven. "Such a worrier!" she chastised herself. "Ease up and enjoy yourself a bit, will you?" She opened her laptop, logged on, and distracted herself with reading her work email. There were a couple of questions from students that she could answer quickly, a request for an assignment extension from another student that took a little longer, a reminder about a job candidate coming in that she'd forgotten about, and several other college- and department-wide messages that she could just skim. Teaching at a local university gave her the luxury of having a more flexible schedule than most jobs. This semester, she normally went to campus only on Mondays, Wednesday, and Fridays, when she was scheduled to teach. Even though it was a Tuesday, she'd decided to go in to her office anyway, to have some quiet time to grade an assignment and have lunch with her colleague Marta. James had an editorial job with a publisher downtown, but usually telecommuted from home. They were respectful of each other's space and schedules while working from home, but Caroline sometimes appreciated the "alone time" her campus office afforded her.

Caroline shot off a quick email to Marta: "Sorry, I have to cancel lunch today. Plans changed and I won't be coming in like I'd intended; hope to see you tomorrow." She then turned her attention to the stack of papers that represented the first graded essay assignment for two sections of Freshman English. She pushed a lock of greying blonde hair behind one ear and got to work. Soon she was lost in marking errors and commenting upon the students' writing; she was about a third of the way through the stack when she looked up and could see the New York skyline in the distance. They'd be there soon! She'd forgotten her sense of anxiety and was now looking forward to her spur-of-the-moment getaway to the big city.

The bus heaved to a halt in front of the Jacob Javits Center and the passengers started to gather their things and exit the bus. Caroline loaded everything into her backpack and headed down the back staircase of the upper deck then forward to the front exit. She stepped off the bus into a cool, crisp early fall day in New York: there was a nip in the air but the sun was shining brightly and the day seemed full of infinite possibilities. Caroline toyed with the idea of heading toward Central Park, but opted instead to walk south. It would be a beautiful day to just wander through the city, feeling all the hustle and bustle in the streets, and exploring anything that caught her eye. She remembered visiting a great bulk candy shop somewhere on the Lower East Side, near Orchard Street. She couldn't remember exactly where it was, but she set that in mind as a vague goal for her wanderings.

For the next hour she ambled south, peering in shop windows, eavesdropping on conversations in the streets, and feeling generally alive and free. She bought some roasted almonds from a street vendor to munch along the way. At times, she felt a bit chilled and wished she had brought a jacket with her; it was cooler here than it had been in Philadelphia when she'd left home. After a while, she turned to the west and started exploring some side streets she was unfamiliar with, finally stopping to rest on wrought iron bench outside of an apartment building. The street was surprisingly quiet, but it was a mostly residential street in the middle of the day. An alleyway opening across the street caught her attention and made her remember the "shuts of Shrewsbury" walking tour she'd been on in England a few years earlier. The tour guide had taken them down the dark and winding, almost hidden, "shuts" or alleys of the old medieval city.

"I wonder what New York alleys are like," she thought. "I don't think I've ever been in one." Deciding to embark on a new experience, she walked across the street and into the alley, finding herself in an almost maze of passages between buildings on adjacent blocks and half-blocks in between. It was fun to be "off the beaten path" of the busy city, making her way past garbage cans and the occasional locked bicycle, and looking up at the fire escapes and small balconies that dotted the higher floors of some of the buildings. She could see laundry fluttering in a few places and some potted plants that waited vainly for the sun in the dark alley. On one second-story fire escape, an orange tom cat was dozing. He opened one eye as Caroline passed, quickly assessed her as "not a threat" and went back to sleep.

Caroline skipped across side streets into the next series of alleys, and after a while she could tell that the area she was now in was more commercial than residential. There were bigger dumpsters in the alleys, wooden pallets leaning against buildings, plastic buckets full of cooking grease and rotting vegetable scraps, and stacks of empty waxed boxes. The smells were more pungent. She turned down a half-block alley that seemed to have fewer restaurants, just dotted with dumpsters and fire escapes. She was half-way down the alley when a girl came tearing around the corner from a side street, yelling "Run!"

At first Caroline wasn't sure what she was seeing. The figure was dressed in bright red and yellow plaid pants, a loose black sweater pocked with holes and runs, and black Doc Marten boots. Her head sported a wild nest of brownish white-girl dreds that seemed to be bouncing in every direction at once as she ran. It briefly flashed in Caroline's mind that "they must be filming a movie," but she knew she hadn't seen any signs of that. Caroline quickly moved out of the middle of the alley, next to a dumpster, and felt the metal door behind her jiggle as her backpack hit against it. It was one of those double metal doors meant for making deliveries, that opened to the outside and had no outer door handles; Caroline could tell that at least one side was unlocked based on its movement. Reacting solely on instinct rather than logical thought, she jumped forward and grabbed the girl as she approached.

"No!" shouted the girl, struggling against her.

"Shhhh!" hissed Caroline in response. She pulled the girl toward the door, holding her close with her right arm while she pried the unlocked side of the metal door open with her

She was half-way down the alley when a girl came tearing around the corner from a side street, yelling "Run!"

left. She shoved the girl inside, who lost balance and fell to the floor. Caroline pulled the door closed after them as quickly and quietly as possible. It was dark inside, unlit except for a yellow security light in a wire cage that was visible through a doorway on the right. It provided enough dull light that Caroline could see a sliding bolt at the top of the door. She pushed it into place.

"What the fuck?" snarled the girl on the floor.

Caroline responded only with a finger to her lips and a soft "Shhhh!" Seconds later they heard running in the alley outside, large, pounding footsteps, and men shouting.

"Where'd she go?"

"Dunno!"

"You go left, I'll go right!"

The running and pounding receded.

"Those fuckers!" exclaimed the girl.

Caroline sat down on the floor beside her, grasping the girl's arm. "We have to be quiet," she whispered. "They may be coming back."

Within a few minutes they were back, toppling over garbage cans and pounding on doors as they moved back down the alley. The two women held their breath as they heard the men getting closer. One of them pounded violently on the metal door they had just come through, and Caroline put her hand over the girl's mouth to stop her from yelling. They could hear the lid of the dumpster next to the door being opened and slammed shut again, and a man's voice calling out "Not here!" The heavy footsteps receded down the alley in the direction they'd originally come from.

"We have to be quiet and wait here," Caroline whispered again to the girl, who nodded in the semi-darkness. They appeared to be in a warehouse or some sort of a storage area, with lots of stacked boxes and wooden crates on pallets. Caroline could make out an industrial mop bucket and mop in the corner across from them, with a stack of brooms and snow shovels and other implements behind it. She couldn't even guess what kind of business this could be, but she wondered if anyone else was in the building. It was one more reason to try to keep the girl quiet.

Caroline couldn't really tell what the girl looked like as they sat on the floor against a stack of boxes to the right of the door. Even if she couldn't see her well, Caroline had no trouble smelling the girl. It wasn't the smell of sweat from the exertion of running, it was the deep-seated funk of a crusty punk, a type Caroline was familiar with from her West Philadelphia neighborhood. They openly rejected the concepts of soap and shampoo and deodorant, seemed to never shower, and took pride in not washing their clothes, which soon developed a greasy sheen. Despite the lack of hygiene, these rebellious types were secretly some of Caroline's favorites; she admired both their consistency and fortitude. She'd meet them sometimes at the local food co-op or run into them at community group meetings, but they rarely showed up in her classrooms. Higher education was apparently also something to be generally rejected, although Caroline would argue that they took this particular form of political correctness too far.

The two women sat there in the semi-darkness for what seemed like an eternity, the girl's heavy breathing finally slowing to normal and Caroline's spiked adrenaline evening out somewhat. She wracked her brain for what to do next, and wondered what she'd gotten herself into, inserting herself into this situation. But she also wondered what would have happened if she hadn't dragged the girl inside. What would those men have done to her? What would they have done to Caroline if she'd stumbled into their path as well?

She briefly considered if the girl could be a thief, chased for shoplifting or some other petty crime, but quickly dismissed the idea. What she'd heard from the men in the alley didn't seem like the words or actions of wronged shopkeepers. The vibe they gave off was dark and heavy, even dangerous. She had no idea what the story of this chase was, but her sympathies were naturally with the hunted, not the hunters.

"Why were you running from them?" Caroline asked quietly, finally breaking the silence.

The girl followed her cue and responded intently but in a low voice. "They're bastards!" she said. "They're traffickers!"

Caroline felt a shock wave go through her. "Are they trafficking you?" she asked, lightly touching the girl's arm.

"No!" the girl responded, her voice sounding irritated and starting to rise.

Caroline heard a noise that sounded like it was coming from the other end of the building, filtering down the hallway.

"We should leave," she whispered to the girl. "But you owe me an explanation. Do you promise not to run when we get outside?"

"OK," said the girl, dredlocs bobbing.

Caroline stood up, pulled her backpack back on, then went to the door and quietly unbolted the side that they had entered through earlier. She and the girl stepped into the alley, which even in its shadows seemed bright compared to the darkness they'd been sitting in. Caroline pushed the door shut behind them.

"Let's go this way," Caroline said, holding on to the girl's arm and moving in the direction she had originally entered the alley from, in what now seemed like a lifetime ago.

She got a better look at the girl in the daylight—she was thin and pale but seemed healthy. Her face was lightly dotted with freckles and she had clear blue eyes. She wasn't carrying a bag or backpack or anything, which struck Caroline as odd; most people, especially women, carried something for the "stuff" they brought with them.

A disturbing thought suddenly crossed Caroline's mind. This girl was, if nothing else, conspicuous. "If those men are looking for you, maybe we should try to make you harder to find?" she tentatively suggested.

"What do you mean?" asked the girl.

"Well, those pants are simply screaming 'HERE I AM!' for one thing," said Caroline.

"I like these pants," the girl replied defensively.

"I do, too," said Caroline, only partly lying. "But maybe we should try to get you looking a bit different, to be on the safe side. There's a thrift store I saw earlier, right up this block."

Caroline had noticed the thrift store before, when she was crossing the street between alleys. She turned up the block and the girl followed, trailing her into the store. A sad-looking woman in her thirties sat behind a service counter and smiled at them. The place was full of overstuffed racks of clothing, shelves of knick-knacks, and some larger pieces of furniture in the back. Yellowed florescent lighting units swung from the ceiling overheard. Christian rock music blared from a tinny sound system. The girl started rapidly pawing through a rack of clothes, almost like she was looking for something specific. Caroline decided not to hover, and found a rack on the other side of the shop that had women's coats and jackets on it. The chill outside had been bothering her, so she might as well add another layer.

Caroline tried on several things, looking at herself in a full-length mirror attached to the wall. She settled on a grey trench coat with double-breasted buttons and a belt tie. She headed back to the service desk, arriving just as the girl emerged from the dressing room next to it. She was wearing non-descript black pants, a dark brown shirt with some sort of subtle black print that was almost indiscernible, and a cheap faux leather motorcycle jacket. "How's this?" she asked Caroline.

"You look great. You just need a hat." A hat rack was on the other side of the service desk and Caroline looked through it, pleased to find a man's XL black beret there. She plopped it onto the girl's head and stuffed the dreds sticking out the front up into the beret. The others she pulled behind the girl's ears, where they stuck out in back like a bushy ponytail. The hairstyle was undisguisable, but the hat modified the look and made the girl's face look different—less hidden, more feminine.

"Can we just wear these things out with us?" Caroline asked the woman working there.

"Sure," she replied. She came around from the counter with a pair of scissors and started snipping tags off of the various items of clothing. Then she went back behind the counter and started adding the amounts up on a grimy calculator.

The girl returned to the dressing room and came back out with her old clothes rolled in a bundle. She stuck her hand in the plaid pants' pocket and pulled out some crumpled bills and loose change, scattering them on the counter.

"Oh, no," said Caroline, quickly. "I've got this."

"OK," said the girl, sounding a bit unsure if she should be accepting the offer. But she acquiesced quickly and added on a "Thanks."

"Do you want to, um, get rid of those things?" asked Caroline, gesturing to the bundle of clothes the girl was holding.

"No way!" responded the girl with a dark look. "I *like* these clothes!"

"I can put those in a bag for you," the woman behind the counter said kindly, pulling out a used plastic bag from under the counter. To Caroline she said, "$36.65."

Caroline fished her wallet out of her backpack and pulled out a couple of $20 bills. The woman handed the plastic bag to the girl, who rolled her eyes when she saw the name on it. "Seriously? Barney's?" she complained.

"It's just a bag," said Caroline, waiting while the woman behind the counter dug through a cash box for her change. She took her change back with a "Thank you!" and a meaningful look.

Back out on the street, the two women lingered tentatively on the sidewalk in front of the store. "Let's go somewhere and talk," said Caroline. "I'm starving—what about you?"

The girl grunted noncommittally and Caroline pointed to a small diner further up the street. "Let's just duck in there for a while."

When they walked in, the older woman behind the cash register next to the door said, "Sit anywhere," and waved her hand toward the interior. Caroline led them to a small booth beside a window looking out on the side street, pulled off her backpack and plopped down on one side of the table while the girl sat at the other, pushing her plastic Barney's bag against the window.

A waitress came by and slammed down two plastic glasses of ice water, and dropped a couple of sticky, plastic-coated menus at the end of the table. "I'll be right back, ladies," she said.

The lunch hour rush was over and the restaurant had only a few of the other tables occupied. Caroline and the girl stared at the menus in silence for a few minutes before the girl announced, "I'm a vegan."

"Of course you are," thought Caroline. She didn't reply, but immersed herself in the flapping paper clipped to the menu detailing the specials of the day. Her mind eventually turned back to the girl and the strange situation she'd stumbled into. She wondered what she needed to do next. Should she just buy them lunch and then get back on the bus to Philly? Should she go to the police? Or was there something that was more "in between" these extremes?

The waitress returned with a brusk "What can I git cha?"

"House salad," said the girl. "No egg. No bacon. Extra tomatoes. Vinaigrette on the side."

"I'll have the Rubin," said Anna. "Chips, not fries."

"Meat is murder," said the girl under her breath as the waitress walked away.

"What?" asked Caroline.

"Nothing."

Caroline sighed. The girl looked to be in her early twenties, about the age of many of her students. But she didn't really remind her of her students, most of whom seemed soft, tentative, and a little lost in comparison. This girl had harder edges to her, and exuded a confidence and willfulness that betrayed a maturity beyond her years. A couple of years ago, when she'd turned forty, Caroline suddenly realized that she was old enough to have grown children the age of the students she was now teaching. She and James never had children, opting instead to concentrate on their careers and to spend their money on their own interests. She sometimes wondered what it would be like having a nearly adult child in her life, and the girl in front of her provided an entirely new perspective on that. She realized that anyone looking at them sitting here now might easily mistake them for mother and daughter.

"I don't believe we've been properly introduced," Caroline said, breaking the silence. "I'm Caroline Wilson. I teach college English at a university in Philadelphia and I'm actually just here in the city for the day. What's your name?"

"They call me 'Mugwump,'" replied the girl.

Caroline hoped that her face didn't betray any reaction to the Burroughs reference. "OK, Mugwump. Nice to meet you. Can you tell me what the hell that was back there?"

"Those were some grade-A assholes who seriously need to be taken down, chasing me. With guns. I don't think you would have seen that."

Caroline gulped. She hadn't seen that, in fact she hadn't seen the assholes at all. And luckily, they hadn't seen her, either. But here she was, sitting in a diner with the girl they were after.

"But why were they chasing you?" she asked. "You said earlier that they were traffickers. Were they trafficking you?"

"No, I already told you that."

Caroline waited for her to say more. "They're not trying to traffick me," she continued. "They're trafficking women and girls from Thailand, and some other places in southeast Asia."

"But, why . . . how do you know?" asked Caroline, causing the girl to roll her eyes. "Maybe it would help if you just told me the whole story, starting at the beginning."

She sat there and listened while Mugwump spun her story out. She'd been a student at Hampshire College in Vermont ("hippie school," Caroline mentally registered), majoring in "Ag" because "food is important." But a trip to Thailand to study innovations in rice farming changed the direction of her interests. She'd been disgusted by the sex tourism she saw in Bangkok. "It's just a normal part of the economy," she told Caroline. "I'm definitely not opposed to sex work, when the people involved have chosen that and have agency. But most of the people I saw in Bangkok didn't really have a choice. They were young women and children, without an education, being exploited by men who took most of the money made from Western tourists."

After returning to Vermont, Mugwump found that she had a hard time focusing on her studies. A friend invited her to New York and she ended up staying, getting involved in an anarchist collective on the Lower East Side and cooking for their Food Not Bombs program. One night a young Asian woman showed up, obviously hungry and distressed. She had sat at a table by herself, eating and visibly holding back tears. She'd reminded Mugwump of some of the young women she'd seen in Bangkok, so she sat down and tried to talk with her. The girl knew little English and Mugwump had only learned a bit of Thai on her trip, but she was able to find out that the girl was Thai, that her name was Nusara, and that she'd experienced something traumatic. She was frightened and alone in a strange country.

Mugwump brought the girl home with her that night. She was ecstatic to have a shower and wash her hair, and change into some clean clothes that Mugwump gave her. She stayed in Mugwump's room, in a large run-down house shared with a number of other young anarchists, sleeping on a foam

mattress on the floor. The next day, with the help of a Thai/
English dictionary and some drawing paper and a pencil,
Mugwump learned more of Nusara's story.

* * * * *

Nusara had lived in the country on her family's farm. They
were poor, but they had enough to eat from the crops they
grew. She was the oldest in a large family and she'd only gone
to school for a few years, dropping out to help in the family
fields. One day, a well-dressed Thai woman drove up to their
farm in a big car and told her parents that she worked for
a company that could provide a job for Nusara in America,
being a nanny to a rich family's children. It would pay well
and Nusara could send money home. She'd have a chance to
learn English and the company had a scholarship program
that would allow her to take classes and get an education. It
had sounded almost too good to be true, but it had been too
compelling to say "no" to. Nusara was sad to leave her home,
her parents, and her younger siblings, but she was excited
about the prospect of getting a job and being able to help her
family, as well as having the opportunity to see America.

When it was time to leave, the company picked her up in
a van and she traveled across the country, seeing more of her
homeland than she ever had before. But she had suspected that
something was wrong when she wasn't taken to the airport
to fly to America as promised, but rather was brought to an
industrial port. She was forced onboard a rusty, commercial-
looking boat, along with the other young women that the
van had picked up along the way. Her passport and suitcase
were taken away from her, and she was put in a hold with
about twenty other women. All of the women were crying

and wailing, knowing they were in a bad situation that was only going to get worse.

There were only a few small windows in the hold, and the air was stale and fetid. There were plastic buckets to use as toilets and a few straw mats on the floor for sleeping. The food was bad and there was not enough of it. There was no water to wash with and even clean drinking water was in short supply. Despite the hardships, the women had banded together. They made sure that food was distributed equally. They comforted each other with stories of their homes and families, and their hope to return to them. They fantasized about overcoming the guard when he brought food and turning the boat around to go home, but they never had the means or opportunity to do that.

After what seemed like weeks aboard the ship, it finally came to a stop. They could hear men moving around and a lot of talking on deck. In the middle of the night, the hold was opened and the women were brought out on deck, the first time they'd been in fresh air since they'd left Thailand. They were forced to climb down a long, swaying ladder on the side of the boat, which Nusara recalled with terror. At the bottom of the ladder, she was grabbed by men who pulled her onto a motor boat where she was chained together with a group of the other women. Once all of the women were onboard, the smaller boat took them to a dark dock, where they climbed out of the boat and were herded into the back of an enclosed delivery truck.

The truck drove for an hour or more, and then they were unloaded in the alley behind some sort of commercial building and forced into a basement room. The same pattern of not enough food and not enough hygiene continued for several days. Occasionally one of the women was dragged out of the room and then would return later, crying and holding together ripped clothing. Everyone knew what was happening but no one talked about it. They tried to comfort the abused woman who returned but secretly gave thanks that it hadn't been them. One night, Nusara was awakened by a man grabbing her wrist and dragging her out of the room. Her turn had arrived, and yet it had also proven to be a salvation of sorts.

She was taken upstairs and shoved into an office. The man locked the door behind them. There was an old chair in front of a metal desk that was covered with papers, and some metal filing cabinets that the man shoved her up against, bruising her back against the metal handles. He pulled at her shirt, running his right hand over her breasts while holding her shoulder with his left. But then the phone rang. He pulled Nusara up close against him, holding his hand over her mouth while he answered the phone. She knew that the time to act was now or never. While the man was talking, she grabbed a metal stapler off the desk and smashed it against his head. He cried out and dropped the phone, as she wiggled out of his grasp. She kicked him as hard as she could between his legs, just like her friend Nin had showed her back home. The man doubled over and Nusara unlocked the office door and ran. She had no idea of where she was, but see saw a white and red sign over a door at the end of the hall and ran for it. The door opened when she pushed the metal bar and an alarm went off. She ran as fast as she could into the night.

The streets she ran through were mostly dark in the commercial area she found herself in. She saw one lit sign a few blocks away, yellow with red and black letters and a funny picture of a sandwich that had a dog's head, feet, and tail. Once she got there, she could see more lights, cars, and people in the blocks ahead, so she ran towards them. She did not even know what city she was in. She walked along the streets, not knowing where to go. Eventually she got tired, and curled up beside some steps in a back alley and slept for a while. She awakened early the next morning and spent the day walking the streets. She didn't know enough English to speak to anyone, and she did not see anyone who looked like they could speak her language. She had no money and nothing other than the clothes she was wearing. For the next few days, she scavenged food from garbage cans and dumpsters behind restaurants, and slept on the street. It was purely by chance that, on her fourth night on the street, she walked past the storefront hosting Food Not Bombs and recognized the words "Free Food." The smells coming from inside enticed her to enter.

Nusara kept insisting "Find Sheriff" after she had communicated her story to Mugwump; it was as if she had seen too many American westerns and thought that would solve the problem. "No Sheriff" was Mugwump's repeated reply. Once she understood what had happened to Nusara, Mugwump wanted to find the place where she had been held. The Thai girl was understandably not eager to return there and seemed genuinely unsure of where she had actually been. But Mugwump brought her to the Food Not Bombs storefront and started having her walk around the area with her. Nusara hid inside the hood of a sweatshirt Mugwump had given her, trying to remain unseen. Occasionally she pointed out things that she thought she recognized. On the second day of doing this, they found the yellow and red sandwich shop sign with the distinctive picture of the "hot dog" dog on it. Nusara was able to indicate the direction she'd come from when she first saw the sign, and where she'd turned to get

On the second day of doing this, they found the yellow and red sandwich shop sign with the distinctive picture of the "hot dog" dog on it.

onto that street. She was very scared to be this close to her captors, so Mugwump told her to go home and she did the rest of the reconnaissance by herself. After some scouting in the area that Nusara had indicated, she narrowed the possible location down to a few buildings on a side street a few blocks up from the sandwich shop.

She started walking by these buildings every day, as often as she could manage it, sometime lingering on the corner while pretending to look at her phone. Occasionally she'd see men coming and going from one of the buildings, and after awhile some of them started to notice her as well. Their reactions went from scowling to open abuse and threats, so she tried to keep her observations more at a distance and started coming more often at night. Late one afternoon, she noticed a large enclosed truck parked halfway up on the sidewalk behind the building. It looked like the type of truck she imagined Nusara and the other women being put in when they were transferred from the boat to here. She decided to risk coming closer to the building again and walked down the alley toward the truck. She first walked past the truck, looking in the side mirror to see no one in the cab of the truck, and glancing inside as she passed, just to make sure. Seeing no one there, she continued to the end of the block and then doubled back. Looking carefully around for signs of anyone near the buildings, she banged sharply on the side of the truck with her fist. She felt and heard the reverberation, but it seemed hollow and there was no sound in response. She left the block quickly, vowing to return after dark.

After finishing a shift at Food Not Bombs, she headed back over to the warehouse district. She was dressed all in black, including an oversized hoodie that she wore with the hood up, concealing her face like a Sith Lord. She had a set of brass knuckles in her pocket that she wasn't entirely sure she knew how to use, but they made her feel more secure. She stationed herself in the alley a couple of blocks up from the parked truck, hidden as much as possible by some garbage cans and a metal stairwell. She leaned against the wall of the building, staying as quiet and still as possible, blending into the shadows. She was standing there for hours, the cool night air helping to keep her awake and alert. Her persistence paid off a little after three a.m., when she saw two men emerge from the building and head to the truck. They unlocked the back of the truck and opened the doors, glancing up and down the street. Mugwump had held her breath, not daring to move enough to even breathe. The men returned to the building but emerged soon after with two others, hustling a group of women into the back of the truck. They slammed the doors shut and Mugwump swore she heard the click of a lock. There was some muffled conversation and two of the men got into the cab of the truck and the driver started the engine. The two men left behind returned into the building as the truck drove off. Mugwump was terrified that she might be spotted in the headlights, or that the truck would drive past her and she'd be seen, but luckily it turned at the end of the first block, before getting to her.

She waited a few more minutes, glued to her post in the alley, until she was convinced that the truck had really left and that the men inside the building weren't coming back outside. Then she sprinted away from the building as fast as she could, her hands balled into fists and her mind overcome by rage. She hadn't stopped them from taking the women; she couldn't stop them from taking the women. She was one woman in an alley with a set of brass knuckles and they were four muscular men armed with guns. On one of her earlier reconnaissance forays, a man outside the building had grinned at her as she'd walked past and pulled one side of his jacket open to reveal a holstered pistol at the side of his chest. That was when she'd made the decision to stay further away and observe from a distance. Her logical mind told her there was nothing she could do in the face of such a power imbalance, but she was still enraged by her impotence. She knew that these women and girls were on their way to the next stage of their exploitation: those considered the prettier ones would probably be sent to massage parlors somewhere and the others sold off into slavery at a sweatshop somewhere else.

* * * * *

Mugwump finished her story and finished her salad, pushing the bowl away from her. She locked eyes with Caroline across the table. "That truck I told you I saw? It's parked back on the sidewalk again, *now*. I got caught walking past it this time, and that's why I was being chased when you first saw me."

Caroline swallowed hard. "That's quite the story," she replied. "But I have to ask: if you know what's going on there, why not go to the police? Isn't there some sort of unit or department or something that works on human trafficking?"

Mugwump rolled her eyes. "Honestly, the police?" she countered. "There's no way that they don't already know what's going on, that they're not being paid off to let it happen."

"Hey, I get it," said Caroline. "I'm from Philly and I know the whole 'don't snitch' routine. I understand that dealing with the cops can be worse than dealing with the crooks, but something like this...."

"There's no good solution," broke in Mugwump. "Can't deal with the cops. Can't deal with the traffickers. But I've been working on a plan to try to force them to deal with each other. Problem is, with that truck in the alley, I have to move *now*. If the pattern holds true, it'll be gone with another group of women tonight."

"OK, well, what do you mean? What's the plan?"

Mugwump's eyes narrowed as she considered Caroline across the table. "It's complicated. All I can say is that time is of the essence…and maybe, I could use someone like you to help."

Caroline silently considered the younger woman's words for a few minutes. What kind of dangerous nonsense was she potentially getting herself drawn into? Was this another one of the anxiety scenarios she'd imagined earlier, but one that was so improbable that she couldn't have even conjured it up? Yet she felt drawn to trying to help this woman, who seemed so smart and tough and headstrong, but who also seemed to be teetering on the edge of something very dangerous.

"Alright," she finally said, deciding to test the waters. "What kind of help do you need?"

"I don't want to explain it here. Can you come meet my friend Jello at the Infoshop? It's a few blocks from here."

"Yes, I suppose so," Caroline said tentatively. She pulled out her phone and looked at the time. "2:30. I was hoping to catch the bus back to Philly by three, but I can work out a way to stay longer if I need to."

"Well, let's go then," said Mugwump, standing up and grabbing her Barney's bag.

Caroline looked at the check that the waitress had left on the table, pulled a couple of bills from her wallet and handed it all to the cashier at the front, with a "Keep the change," as she rushed to follow Mugwump out of the door.

They headed back down the sidewalk in the direction they'd come from. "I'm curious," said Caroline, "how is Nusara doing now?"

"No idea," responded Mugwump gruffly. "She totally disappeared after staying at my place for about two weeks."

"Oh, I'm sorry." Caroline was hoping she wasn't opening a wound, but couldn't contain her curiosity. "What do you think happened to her?"

"Dunno. Maybe she did finally figure out how to go to the cops. The idea of 'the sheriff' kept coming up with her, no matter how many times I shot it down."

"Ummm," Caroline murmured in response.

"Actually, it might have been the best thing. Maybe if she went to them, they'd have turned her over to ICE and best result would be having her deported back to Thailand so she could go home."

"Right, that might be best."

"Worst case would be that one of the traffickers spotted her, and that she'd be right back where she left. Or dead."

Caroline really didn't want to think about that possibility. "Could she have just gone off on her own?"

"Might have. But I think that's the most unlikely explanation. She was so grateful to me, and seemed like she'd be so lost on her own. I really can't imagine it. I don't think she would have left of her own will without telling me, or without at least saying good-bye."

They'd turned left and were heading down a street that Caroline was unfamiliar with. A few blocks later, they halted in front of an unassuming brownstone with a black painted railing in front. Almost invisible from the street, there was a hand-drawn sign in the basement window at ankle level that read: "INFOSHOP Come On Down."

Mugwump led Caroline down some steep steps to the basement area. Once they got inside, it was larger and better lit than Caroline would have expected. There was a bulletin board with an array of flyers tacked to it and a rack of pamphlets near the door where they entered. DIY wooden bookshelves filled with books lined the sides of two walls and there was a beat up four-drawer filing cabinet at the end of one of them with a sign declaring "ZINES!!!" A small table at the end of the other held a domestic coffeemaker, cans of coffee, a collection of chipped mugs, and an empty can labeled "$." A worn rag rug covered the middle of the floor and mismatched second-hand seating was scattered throughout. A thin young Black man in greasy jeans and an unbuttoned camouflage shirt over a dark blue t-shirt was slumped in a worn easy chair, one leg draped over an arm of the chair, reading a comic book. A pale young white man with curly red hair dressed in all black was sprawled in a beanbag chair under the window, reading a book. Caroline couldn't quite catch the title, but there was a photograph of an atomic bomb blast on the cover. They both glanced up without much interest when the two women entered.

"Hey, Mugwump."

"What's up, Wump?"

"Hey, guys," said Mugwump in reply. "Is Jello here?"

"Yeah, he's in the back."

"Come on," Mugwump said to Caroline, leading her through a doorway in the far wall that was covered with a piece of cloth and had a "Staff Only" sign above it. They entered a dark room a little larger than the front room, cluttered with stacks of miscellaneous boxes. Some rusty metal shelving units with old paint cans, random tools, and other objects leaned against one wall, and some large paper mâché puppet heads were stacked in one corner. A makeshift office was built out from the far corner of the room, and a line of light showed at the bottom of its closed door. They headed there and Mugwump rapped on the door. "Jello?" she called out.

"Yeah," came a voice within the office. "Come on in."

Mugwump opened the flimsy door of the office and Caroline followed her inside. The cramped space held a couple of desks stacked with papers, a couple of filing cabinets, and a messy pile of cardboard boxes in one corner. A man in who appeared to be older than Mugwump, probably in his mid-thirties, was seated at one of the desks. He had large black-framed glasses, dark hair, and a wispy beard and moustache. He read a bit "hipster" to Caroline with his green knit hat, plaid shirt, blue jeans, and brown work boots. Posters and stickers with radical messages adorned the walls of the office, including a somewhat dated poster with a picture of George W. Bush and the words "Stop Me Before I Kill Again" and an oversized yellow post-it note proclaiming "Are You Fucking Kidding Me?" A fluorescent unit overhead and a desk lamp provided strong lighting in the small room.

"Hey, Mugwump," said the man, and noticing Caroline, "Hello."

"Caroline, this is Jello Ravachol," said Mugwump. "Jello, this is Caroline from Philadelphia."

"Hello, Caroline from Philadelphia," echoed Jello.

"Hello," said Caroline, suddenly feeling a bit shy and out-of-place.

He gestured toward the other desk in the office and offered, "Have a seat." Mugwump pulled the chair around to face the other desk, and motioned to Caroline to sit. She shoved some papers aside on the desktop and perched there herself.

"Jello, they almost got me this time, man!" she blurted out. "They were coming after me with *guns and everything*!"

"They were…what?" asked Jello, confused. "Wait, slow down." Then he turned to Caroline. "*Who* are you, again?"

"I'm sorry," said Caroline. "I'm just someone from Philadelphia who happens to be in town for the day…." She was starting to feel like she really didn't belong here and once again pressed down a wave of fear that she was potentially getting into something way over her head.

"She saved me," broke in Mugwump. "She pulled me inside a building and helped me hide until they went away. I swear, Jello, they're planning a move. The truck is in the alley and it has to be today!"

Jello put up his hand. "Just…stop." He let out a heavy, frustrated sigh. "Come talk to me outside." And to Caroline, he said, "Excuse us."

"Oh, I can leave…" Caroline started to protest, but he waved her off.

"It's ok, we'll be right back." Mugwump followed him out the office door, which they closed behind them.

Left on her own, Caroline scanned more of the posters on the walls and was impressed with the variety of causes they espoused ("Support Indigenous Rights" "Workers Rights Are Human Rights" "Black Lives Matter") and the humor that many of them expressed ("Feeling Sad and Depressed? You Might Be Suffering From Capitalism" "Is It Gay In Here, Or Is It Just Me?"). She couldn't resist the temptation to peek at a few of the papers on the desk, noting some invoices from radical bookstores, an events calendar, and some scrawled incomprehensible phone messages. She could barely hear the muffled voices of the two in the other room, who were having an intense conversation if not a full-blown argument.

Occasionally, she'd catch entire sentences when one of them raised their voice: "But how do you *know*?" from Jello, and "Can't you just trust me on this?" from Mugwump.

Caroline almost jumped when the door re-opened. Mugwump and Jello came in and took their earlier seats, and Jello turned his chair to face Caroline head on.

"Listen, lady, no offense, but…can you provide some sort of proof of who you actually are?"

Caroline bridled a bit at being called "lady" but said "Um, sure" and unzipped her backpack. She pulled out her wallet and produced her drivers' license. "I live in West Philadelphia," she explained. She next produced her faculty ID and said, "I teach in the English Department here." She pulled her backpack open wider and produced a sheaf of student essays. "I was grading papers on my way up, on the bus."

Jello examined the IDs that were produced and seemed especially interested in the student papers. Caroline suppressed a bit of a smile. It's easy enough to make fake IDs, she thought, but forging student papers like this would take a mastermind. Jello seemed to relax a bit after this interrogation, and Caroline felt like she'd passed a test.

"OK," said Jello, handing Caroline back her things. "What's going on, Wump? What's the plan?"

"We have to move sooner rather than later," Mugwump said intensely. "If we don't do it now, anyone they've got there now is lost and I can't fucking *stand* the thought of that! And we may not have another opportunity for weeks."

"Are you sure it wouldn't it be better to wait until night?" asked Jello.

"No. It's better to go now, in broad daylight. It's more obvious, and there will be more witnesses."

"Yeah, more witnesses. That's what I'm afraid of; more chances of getting caught."

"More witnesses to what's actually going on there, and more of a chance they'll have to actually break this thing up. It's the only way this is going to work!"

Jello's forehead creased in thought. "Hmm…you may be right."

Caroline sat silently, listening to the exchange and trying to figure out what exactly was going on. She didn't feel comfortable asking questions just yet, and decided to just hang back and observe what unfolds.

Jello shifted in his chair. "What about her? What's the deal with that?"

"She'll be the one to check the front and give the signal. We have to get the timing down, but she walks by, stops in front, and gives the signal if the light is on."

Caroline assumed that the "she" being discussed was her and decided now was the right time to enter the conversation. "Excuse me," she said. "Could you give me some information about what it is you're talking about, and how it involves me?"

They both turned to look at her. Mugwump locked eyes with her and said simply, "We're going to bomb them."

Visions of stereotypical "bomb-throwing anarchists" passed through Caroline's mind; in fact, a black-and-red graphic image of one leered down at her from one of the posters on the wall. "Bomb them?" she repeated. "Are you sure that's a good idea?"

"I've thought about it, Caroline," said Mugwump. "I've thought about it *a lot*. I really believe it's the only way we're going to be able to end this."

Caroline considered the two in front of her. Mugwump had already impressed her as an intelligent young woman with strong convictions. But she was young, and working with young adults had taught Caroline that they don't always think things through clearly or make the best choices. She knew less about Jello but he also struck her as someone who was intelligent and committed to his ideals. Still, she felt the need to be the proverbial "adult in the room."

"At the risk of betraying my own political incorrectness again," she said, "I have to ask: why not go to the police? Why not try to tip off whoever's in charge of anti-trafficking?"

"Because it won't work!" shot back Mugwump, the frustration starting to rise in her voice. "Tipping off the cops is the same thing as tipping off the traffickers. I know the local police have to be in on it. These guys could never be operating so openly like this without the cops being paid to ignore it."

"It's true," confirmed Jello. "There's a lot going on in this city that shouldn't be, because there's too many corrupt cops on the take letting it happen."

Caroline thought about what they said. She knew that there had to be corruption in the Philadelphia police department as well; occasionally she'd see a news report that indicated this or she heard some sort of rumor. But largely the whole concept was totally outside of her normal day-to-day reality. She had her middle-class home, her middle-class job, and her middle-class husband and friends. These young people were talking about an aspect of city life that she believed existed, but that was invisible to her in her own ordinary life in Philadelphia. But that didn't make it any less real.

"OK," she conceded, "but why bombing? What's that going to accomplish?"

"It's going to force it into the public's face," replied Mugwump. "It's going to mean that not just the cops are going to show up, but the firefighters and the medics are going to show up as well. Gawkers who want to see what's happening are going to be hanging around, and the press is going to show up. They'll be forced to publicly acknowledge what's going on and do something about it."

"Well, I have to admit that makes sense," said Caroline. "But you mentioned medics and if you plan on bombing this place, isn't there a real chance that someone might get hurt? How would you feel if that happened?"

"If we got some of the traffickers, believe me, I'm not going to feel bad about it," said Mugwump.

"What we have planned shouldn't be that big and the placements will be made to create the most disruption but with the lowest risk of human harm," explained Jello. "We're really not out to hurt anyone."

"'Shouldn't be that big'?" repeated Caroline. "Are you sure of that?"

"As sure as I can be of anything," said Jello. "I mean, we haven't been stupid enough to test this out anywhere, but in theory it should work."

"Hmmm, 'in theory,'" said Caroline. "What if the theory is wrong? Suppose the whole place goes up in a giant fireball and the women you're trying to help are trapped in there? What then?"

"Then I'd feel really, really bad," said Mugwump glumly. "But I trust Jello to know what he's doing and I'm willing to take that risk; I think it's actually a pretty small one."

"It's meant to be a small, targeted attack, not a massive bombing; we don't want to attract *too much* attention," explained Jello. "There's also a fire station four blocks away. We'll have someone checking to make sure that they're not already out on call before we make our move. They should be able to arrive quickly and deal with the situation before it gets out of control."

"Well, that's reassuring," said Caroline, although she was only partially reassured. "So, what exactly is the deal? What do you want from me in all of this?"

"We need someone who's able to get eyeballs on the place without seeming suspicious. It's simple, really: just stop out front and signal if the office light is on," said Mugwump. "I've seen it from before: it's always dark in the front of the building, but if someone's there, you can see the office light on, down the hallway."

"But, why me?" asked Caroline. "Can't one of your other friends help with this?"

"My friends all look like me and the cops are—how do I say this?—*aware* of us. If one of us is caught on a surveillance camera, that blows the whole thing open. You're from out of town, you've got plausible deniability, right? You don't know us, you aren't connected with us."

"Right," said Caroline. "We met entirely by accident. But, that's really all you need me to do? Just check to see if a light is on?"

"Exactly. You just walk down the street, stop in front of the building and check to see if the light's on. If it is, you give a signal to Jello, who's behind you down the block, and everything proceeds as planned. Jello signals me on the phone, and then runs past and gets the bomb to the front door. Meanwhile, at the same time, I'm delivering the other bomb to the back door. They should both detonate at around the same time."

"Wait—there are *two* bombs?"

"Yeah, of course, there has to be. We don't want the fuckers to just be able to run out the back."

Caroline sighed. She could get up and walk out now, she told herself. But her body didn't move. On some level it felt almost inevitable that she was there, and that she was going to be involved in this scheme, no matter how dangerous or harebrained it seemed. "Alright," she said finally, "show me what I need to do."

* * * * *

Caroline sat on the park bench near the wharf, two blocks up the street from the warehouse, where Mugwump had instructed her to wait; she'd just leaned over discreetly and loosened the lace on her right shoe. It had been a little less than an hour since she had left the Infoshop via the back alley. She'd slowly ambled in this general direction, continuing to sight-see and doing some minor shopping. Before she'd left, Mugwump had drilled her and Jello on the timing of what they needed to do. Caroline couldn't help but be impressed at how well Mugwump had thought this all through. She explained how to find the park bench and what time Caroline needed to be there by. Caroline knew she had to wait for a text message on the encrypted app that Mugwump had installed on her phone. It would be from their contact, indicating that fire trucks were available at the neighborhood station. If the text didn't come within fifteen minutes, she was free to just leave. If the text did come, she had to walk at a certain pace to be in front of the building at the same time that the other two would be closing in on the target destination.

"What if I get stuck crossing the street?" she'd asked.

"You pick up the pace to make up for it. Once you get up from the bench, start counting. You need to be at the end of the first block by the time you count to fifty-five. But there's some wiggle room. Jello will be coming up behind you and if he sees the signal from you, he'll signal me on the phone app to proceed. He can slow down or speed up if he needs to."

"Well, I don't know how much I'm going to be able to speed up," interjected Jello. His part of the plan was the most difficult and elaborate. He was going to change clothes in a different location, be dressed as a jogger with sunglasses, a knit cap, and a neck gaiter obscuring his identity. Once the bomb was planted, he'd run to another location to put on another set of clothes stashed there. He was at the greatest risk of being identified on surveillance cameras, so care had been taken to find locations where he could do quick changes of clothes out of sight and exit in different directions. Mugwump was most familiar with casing the rear of the building and felt confident of her ability to get in and out of the area with a minimum risk of being seen.

They'd spent time going over the plan again and again. Caroline had to repeat the plan back to Mugwump in exact detail several times in order to prove she understood it completely. They practiced counting at a certain rate and walking (and in Jello's case, running) at a certain pace in the back room of the Infoshop. Caroline had been impressed that Mugwump had worked it all out in such detail. She'd paced the whole route out ahead of time, more than once. She gauged her stride against Caroline's stride, saying "You're taller than me, so you'll cover slightly more ground with each step." She had actually measured Caroline's stride and done math to convert her own numbers into a rate that reflected Caroline's natural pace.

As far as Caroline knew, there were two other people in on the plot. One person who'd text after scoping out the fire station, and another person in their circle who wrote for the anarchist press but had also published articles in more mainstream publications. This person had already spread some rumors among local journalists about possible human trafficking in the area, but lacking any firm leads no one had really followed up on it. But he'd been tipped off to be in the area at this general time and to go to the location if a disturbance involving explosions and sirens was heard. He would start taking photographs as soon as possible, and offer copies to any other media that might show up to cover the incident.

Now Caroline sat on the assigned bench, waiting for the text message to come, or not. She tied to quell the butterflies in her stomach by concentrating on other things—the contrast of the strong sunlight and sharp wind of a beautiful fall day, and the papers in her backpack that still needed grading. Her anxiety unfortunately wasn't lessened by the guilt that kept creeping back into her mind. She'd lied to her husband earlier, and it hadn't just been on of those "little white lies" that sometimes get told in marriages to keep things running smoothly. It had, in fact, been a real whopper.

Before she left the back room of the Infoshop, she knew she needed to call her husband to let him know she'd be coming home late. James had picked up on the third ring, with a "Hello, honey."

"Hi, James," she'd replied. "I'm just calling to let you know I'm going to be running late tonight."

"Oh, really?" he'd said, sounding a bit disappointed. "What's up?"

"Oh, you know, it's just been crazy here. I got caught up in all kinds of conversations and emails, and haven't gotten to half the work I'd planned to get done."

"Sorry to hear that, hon."

"And to top it off," she'd continued. "There's a job candidate here who I'd forgotten about. Elaine was supposed to be one of the people going out to dinner with him tonight, but she called in sick. The dean asked me to take her place and, you know, I can't say 'no' to that!"

"Nah, I guess you can't. But at least you'll get a nice dinner out of it, huh?"

"I suppose. So, anyway, the upshot is just not to expect me anytime soon. Just fix something for yourself tonight, and I'll see you when I see you."

"OK, will do. Have a good time, OK?"

"I'll try! Bye, dear!"

"Bye!"

She'd hung up the phone with mixed emotions. Talking to James had felt so normal, but lying to him hadn't. She knew she'd done the right thing to check in and let him know she'd be coming home late; that was typical and expected. She honestly didn't want him wondering where she was, or worrying about her when she didn't come home by dinner time. But at the same time, she felt really bad for lying to him on this scale. She also started to turn over some of the "what if" scenarios that had been playing in her mind in the bus on the way up. Then, they had just been anxious worries; now, putting herself into this scheme made the chances of something unpleasant happening all the more likely.

After she'd finished the phone call, Mugwump had made her recite the details of the plan one more time to make sure she'd got it. The steps, the sequence, the timing all flowed flawlessly from her lips. Mugwump seemed pleased.

"Great!" Mugwump praised her with a grin. "You've got it!" She led her to the back door so that Caroline could leave unseen by the back alley. Caroline turned at the door to say good-bye and she'd seen that Mugwump's face was quite serious. "Thank you," she'd said, with a depth of sincerity.

"Um, you're welcome?" said Caroline, unsure of the etiquette of a situation like this.

"You're doing the right thing. Really."

"OK. Bye!"

Caroline walked out the door and down the alley for a few blocks before emerging onto one of the streets. She decided that the best thing to do was put the whole situation out of her mind and just behave like normal, continuing to enjoy her day in the city as an out-of-towner. She had about forty-five minutes before she had to be in place, and an alarm was set on her phone to give her a ten-minute warning. Her first stop had been a little storefront bakery that had a couple of small tables with chairs at the front. She'd gotten an éclair and a coffee from the counter and sat at one of the tables to enjoy her snack. She even pulled the student papers out of her backpack and graded a couple of them. It was a little difficult to give them her full attention, but it felt good to her to be at least a bit productive with her work.

After she left the bakery, she went up the street and stopped into a drug store, picking up a few items there. Then she continued walking and window shopping. When the alarm buzzed on her phone in her coat pocket, she knew she had plenty of time to unhurriedly move toward her staging area. She'd turned the alarm off quickly and had continued to walk, casually moving in the direction of the assigned bench.

* * * * *

Now her phone buzzed again as she sat on the bench. She pulled it from her pocket and swiped to open the message on

*Caroline walked out the door and down the alley
for a few blocks before emerging onto one of the streets.*

the special privacy app. "Dinner's ready" said the message. Caroline winched a bit at the dinner reference, but recognized it as the agreed-upon "all clear" signal from Mugwump's contact. She quickly deleted the app from her phone, got up off the bench, and started to walk in the direction of the traffickers' building.

Her mind was in high gear as she walked down the street. She was hyperaware of her surroundings: all of the colors, sounds, and smells of the street bombarded her senses. At the same time, part of her mind was in an oasis, slowly counting out her steps as she moved down the street. It was a consistent rhythm as she counted at the agreed-upon pace, almost meditative. The counting was a sea of calm as all else swirled around her.

She came to the end of the first block at exactly the count that Mugwump had predicted. There was no traffic on the side street, so she easily crossed it with no delay. She proceeded down the target block, still counting, still holding to her rhythm. But another part of her mind was succumbing to an anxiety boarding on panic. She'd already put aside any questions about "Am I doing the right thing?" but now she was wondering if Jello was coming, worrying about if the whole scenario was really unfolding as planned. The target building was coming up on her right and she moved to the side, stopping on the sidewalk near the front window. She was fumbling pulling the phone out of her coat pocket and stopped to look at it where she'd have a clear view through the window. She pretended to scroll through her phone, and as casually as possible glanced through the window. She could see a light coming from a doorway down a darkened hallway.

She leaned over and tied her loosened shoelace, giving the signal to the still unseen Jello. She stood back up and continued walking down the street. After only a few steps, she heard a dull "thump" as something hit the door of the building behind her, and a figure in running gear ran past her. Then, within a few seconds, she heard a loud double blast coming from behind her, the second one closely following on the first, which seemed further away. The concussion threw her to the sidewalk.

What happened next was a confused flurry for her. She felt people helping her up and walking her across the street. She heard sirens, saw a gathering crowd, smelled smoke. Some ambulances arrived and one of the medics cleaned a bloody scrape on her left knee and offered her oxygen. She waved it off with a shake of her head. The medic suggested taking her to the hospital for observation but she refused.

"I'm fine," she remembered saying. "I'm just a little shaken up, that's all."

"Well, rest here for a while, until you're cleared to go," replied the medic.

Firetrucks were on the scene, hoses running. The front window of the building had been broken. Caroline could hear sirens on the block behind them as well. A police cruiser pulled up and an officer got out of the passenger side. He talked to the medic and a young woman with red hair who had been one of the people to help Caroline across the street. They both gestured toward Caroline. She felt herself freezing inside as the officer walked toward her, and her mind was in a haze as he asked her some questions—her name, what she was doing there, if she'd be willing to give a statement.

The thought crossed Caroline's mind that she was being arrested as he led her to the police cruiser and opened the back door for her. "No, I'm not being arrested," she told herself, "I'm just an innocent bystander." The officer got back in the front passenger seat and pulled a clipboard with rumpled papers on it from under the dashboard. Behind the wheel was the officer's partner, a young woman not much older than Mugwump, with chin-length brown hair, looking smart in her uniform. The male officer who'd led Caroline to the car told her both of their names, but they went in one ear and out the other. He asked to see her identification and she reached in her backpack to pull out her wallet and produce her driver's license and university ID. She handed the cards to him with a twisted sense of déjà vu from having done the same thing with Jello less than two hours before. She hoped that she'd manage to pass muster here as well.

The officer examined the IDs and wrote things down on the clipboard, confirming that the information on the cards was current. He asked for her phone number and she gave him both her cell phone and office numbers. Then he asked some routine questions about what she was doing in New York and why she was in this area. She stuck to her story of having come up from Philadelphia for the day, to enjoy the fall weather and to do some shopping. Then he asked her some more specific questions about what she'd seen and experienced in the incident.

"I didn't really see much of anything," she explained. There were a few people on the sidewalk ahead of her, she recalled, and a jogger who passed by her. She didn't remember many details about who they were or what they looked like. She hadn't really seen the jogger, wasn't sure if it had been a man or a woman, but thought that the person had been wearing dark blue, or maybe black. "I'm sorry I can't be of more help," she said.

"That's alright," said the officer taking her statement. "It's a shock to be involved in something like this and that makes it hard to remember specifics. If anything comes to you later, though, give us a call." He handed her a business card over the seat back. "That's the number of the precinct, and I've written my name and the case number on the back."

"OK, thanks," said Caroline, taking the card from him and slipping it into the front zippered pouch of her backpack. "Is that everything?"

"Yeah," said the officer. "We'll call you if we need anything further."

"We're done here," said the officer behind the wheel, "and we're heading back to the precinct. Can we drop you anywhere?"

"Oh, thank you!" said Caroline, feeling a sense of exhaustion setting in. "Could you take me to the Jacob Javits Center? Right now, I just want to get on the bus and go home."

"Sure enough," said the officer as she flipped the car into gear and they moved off. Caroline felt strange riding in the back of a police car. She no longer worried that she was being arrested, but she wondered if anyone else seeing her might think that she had been.

"Um, if you don't mind me asking, do you know what it was that happened back there?" she ventured to ask.

"No, not entirely," said the officer behind the wheel. "Reports coming through on radio indicated that there were arrests made at the back of the building. There was definitely some sort of criminal activity going on there, and it might have been something like an attack from a rival gang."

"Wow," said Caroline, not knowing what more to say.

"Looks like you had the bad luck to be right in the wrong place at the wrong time," added the other officer.

"Yeah, I guess," said Caroline. "Actually, I feel kind of lucky that I got by with just a scrapped knee."

"You're right," agreed the officer. "It could have been a lot worse."

They dropped her at the end of the block near the Javits Center. "Thank you!" she called as she got out of the cruiser, turning to smile and give a little wave as the officers drove off. She stopped at a taco truck parked on the street and bought some tacos to eat on the ride home. Then she found the sandwich board propped on the sidewalk that said "Philadelphia" and stood in line to wait for the bus to take her home.

As she waited, she hugged the trench coat tighter around her. It was now dusk and the temperature had dropped. Despite having the coat, she still felt chilled in the fall evening air but was glad that she at least had it to wear. She stamped her feet on the ground and gazed across the street at the beautiful glass structure of the Javits Center. The cool clarity of the glass front of the building reminded her of an ice sculpture, so it did nothing to take off the chill. She looked at it with the familiar emotions of anger and regret that it tended to provoke in her. The events of the day, crazy as they had been, had already faded somewhat. Now she was just a woman standing on a New York City sidewalk, waiting for a bus.

The bus company representative was working her way down the line that Caroline was standing in. "Should be another ten or fifteen minutes," Caroline heard her tell a person further ahead in line. Caroline continued to hug her coat around her and stamp her feet.

"Philadelphia?" asked the representative when she got to Caroline.

"Yup," replied Caroline, as she swung her backpack down and started to dig for her wallet.

"Twenty dollars," said the representative, "should be about ten minutes."

"Thanks," said Caroline as she exchanged a twenty-dollar-bill for a paper ticket. She pulled her backpack back up onto her shoulders, just as she caught sight of an odd figure walking across the street. The person was wearing a bright orange sweatshirt with the hood up, partially obscuring their face, faded blue jeans, and red high-top sneakers. A small brown paper bag was tucked under one arm, and the figure seemed to be moving directly toward her.

"Oh, no," thought Caroline, as a feeling of panic welled up in her. "What now?"

It was clear to Caroline that this wasn't a figment of a paranoid imagination. The figure was, in fact, making a beeline toward her. She gulped and took a deep breath to try to calm herself down. She had dodged so many bullets today, she thought; could it all finally come crashing down, just as she was about to be safely on her way home?

As the figure drew nearer, Caroline's feelings of concern lessened somewhat. It was Mugwump—but what was she doing here, coming back into contact after everything that had happened today?

"Hey," Mugwump said, stopping on the sidewalk next to Caroline.

"Hey," said Caroline back, not sure what more she could risk saying to this woman.

"I just wanted to, you know, say 'thanks' again, for your help and for being so awesome today."

"There's really no need..." started Caroline, but Mugwump cut her off.

"'K, well, I wanted to give you this," she said as she thrust the brown paper bag into Caroline's hands. "It's from the

Infoshop." Then she reached out to Caroline with one arm for a quick, awkward half-hug.

Caroline was surprised but tried to return the embrace as warmly as she could. She could feel what seemed to be a book in the paper bag she was holding.

"Bye!" said Mugwump, walking a few steps backward down the sidewalk before turning to run into the gathering dark.

"Bye!" Caroline called back, watching the bright orange sweatshirt recede into the night. She pushed the paper bag into the bag from the drugstore just as the bus pulled up and sighed to a stop alongside her.

Caroline had a double seat to herself again on the upper deck of the bus. She'd plopped down, dropping her backpack, the drugstore bag, and the to-go bag of tacos onto the seat beside her. She knew that she needed to grade more student papers, but didn't feel like she could concentrate well enough to consider them fairly. She had classes to teach tomorrow, and she'd just have to tell the students that she'd be a little late with this round of papers. This was the kind of thing that usually created a lot of guilt in Caroline, but right now she had to admit that it was the only reasonable course of action. Grading papers was not her priority after all she'd experienced that day.

As the bus approached the Lincoln Tunnel, she pulled out the paper bag that Mugwump had given her. Filled with curiosity, she took out the hardback book inside. The cover read: *Anarchist Women, 1870-1920* by Margaret S. Marsh. Caroline examined it closely. It had been published a number of decades ago by a university press in Philadelphia, but she had never heard of it. This copy showed signs of much use, with a worn and slightly tattered book jacket and lots of underlining and marginal notes written in the text. She read the blurb on the cover with interest:

> The anarchist-feminists and their ideology possess a significance that extends beyond anarchism and nineteenth-century popular images of it. This book examines the women who espoused anarchism and what they believed, but more importantly it seeks to understand the unique ways in which a group of women responded to the social, sexual, and economic upheavals of the late nineteenth and early twentieth centuries. The antistatist, antiauthoritarian, decentralist visions of the anarchists are an integral part of our intellectual heritage. What the women anarchists tried to do is an important part of the history of the intellectual roots of the women's movement.

Then she opened the book and started to read.

* * * * *

Caroline awoke with a start when the bus came to a halt outside of Philadelphia's 30th Street Station. The driver had turned on all the interior lights and was making an announcement that this was the final stop and to make sure you took all of your belongings with you. Caroline had fallen asleep with the book on her lap, and hurried to put it and the items from the drugstore bag into her backpack. Exiting the bus, she found a trash can and threw away the food bag and the now empty drugstore bag from her New York trip. She briefly considering ditching the trench coat as well, but it was colder in Philly now, too, and she decided to wear it home.

After a quick trolley ride and walking a few blocks back to the house, she was home. James got up from the couch when she came in the front door. "Hi, honey," he said, wrapping her in his arms after she finished locking the door. "I'm glad you're finally home!"

"Me, too!" Caroline replied, with more enthusiasm than she'd intended. "It's been quite a day!"

"Are you hungry at all? There's some leftover stir fry in the fridge if you are."

"No, thanks," said Caroline, remembering both the fact that she was supposed to have been at a fancy faculty dinner and the tacos she'd eaten on the bus while reading. "I'm stuffed!"

James held her at arm's length and considered her. "New coat?" he asked. "I don't think I've seen that before."

"New-old," said Caroline. "I left the house without a jacket this morning and it got colder than I expected, so I ducked into one of the thrift shops downtown and picked this up. Like it?"

James sniffed. "Smells a little…smoky."

"Probably from someone's fire sale," said Caroline, and James chuckled.

"Well, ready to just kick back and watch some TV with me? Glass of wine, maybe?"

The latter sounded tempting, but Caroline shook her head. "Sorry, dear, it's just been such a long, exhausting day for me. I think I'll go take a shower and get to bed early, if you don't mind."

"Suit yourself," said James, settling back down on the couch. "I hope that you get some good rest!"

"Thanks, dear," said Caroline as she headed up the steps, her familiar home suddenly having a somewhat surreal quality to it.

* * * * *

The next day Caroline was back to her usual routine, going into campus to teach her classes and putting in extra time to get caught up on her grading. The trip to New York now seemed unreal, like something she had dreamed and that had soon faded away.

But about a week after her trip, Caroline was in her office at work and decided to log onto her university library's resources and look at the electronic subscription they provided to the *New York Times*. After a little hunting around, she found the article that she was looking for, headlined "Double Bombing at SoHo Industrial Building." The article noted that small bombs had been set off at both the front and rear of the building, that three men inside had been arrested and that two of their associates not on the scene at the time had been tracked down and also arrested, and that sixteen women and girls had been rescued from the basement of the building, presumably from human trafficking. A truck had also been impounded at the scene, and authorities were investigating it to see if they could find clues to a wider trafficking network. There were no arrests made in the bombing itself, but the mayor's office had issued a formal statement that terrorism was not suspected. It was, rather, attributed to "garden variety" criminal activity by the mayor; police detectives welcomed any tips or information. The building was damaged by the bomb blasts and subsequent fires, but only minor injuries were reported, including to a visitor from Philadelphia who happened to be walking past at the time.

Well, there's my claim to fame, thought Caroline. I'm the anonymous visitor…but I guess I'm also the accidental anarchist. She picked up the worn book from her desktop, removed the bookmark, and continued to read.

About the Author

A.R. Melnik is a long-time West Philadelphia resident. All of her trips to New York have been planned in advance.

Enjoyed this story? Read more from Frayed Edge Press...

Literature

Ambushing the Void short stories by James McAdams
*¿Cómo Hacer Preguntas? or How To Make Questions: 69 Instructional
  Poems (in English)* by Daniel Hales
Bellapalma by Jens Bjørneboe; translated by Esther Greenleaf Mürer
Ere the Cock Crows by Jens Bjørneboe; translated and with a
  reconstruction of the play by Esther Greenleaf Mürer
Rape Jokes by Louise MacGregor
Stealing: A Novel in Dreams by Shelly Brivic
The Splooge Factory poety by Christina Springer

History and Politics

*"Do Not Misunderstand Me": The Collected Radical Addresses to the
  Unity Congregation (1888-1891)* by Hugh Owen Pentecost
Jeremiah Hacker: Journalist, Anarchist, Abolitionist by Rebecca
  Pritchard
A Nurse's Story: Medical Missionary in Korea and Siberia, 1915-1920 by
  Delia Battles Lewis

Street Smart Series -- Short Fiction for People on the Go

Full Fare by Jean-Bernard Pouy
Down and Out in Paris, with Cat by R.A. Bolo
The Accidental Anarchist by A.R. Melnik
Stealing MacGuffin by Matthew Kastel
Pele's Domain by Albert Tucher

Visit us at: https://www.frayededgepress.com/